Blasted in

For an instant I thought I had gone blind. Or maybe crazy. I felt like I was being whirled around. Strange noises screamed past my head in the darkness.

Then I began to see things that didn't make any sense: trees shrinking and growing, fires in the sky, rivers of ice flowing to a frozen sea. The world seemed to whirl faster and faster.

Don't miss Bruce Coville's other Camp Haunted Hills books: *How I Survived My Summer Vacation* and *Some of My Best Friends are Monsters*.

Other Books by Bruce Coville

The Monster's Ring

My Teacher is an Alien

Monster of the Year

Available from MINSTREL Books

CAMP Haunted HILLS

The Dinosaur that Followed Me Home

by

Bruce Coville

Illustrated by
John Pierard

A GLC Book

A MINSTREL® BOOK

PUBLISHED BY POCKET BOOKS

New York   London   Toronto   Sydney   Tokyo   Singapore

**For Tripper,
second son of Robert**

A MINSTREL PAPERBACK *ORIGINAL*

A Minstrel Book published by
POCKET BOOKS, a division of Simon & Schuster
1230 Avenue of the Americas, New York, NY 10020

Special thanks to Pat MacDonald for her editorial support.

Cover art by David Dorman
Illustrations by John Pierard
Book Design by Alex Jay/Studio J
Mechanicals by Paula Keller
Typesetting by Jackson Typesetting
Developed by Byron Preiss and Daniel Weiss
Editor: Tisha Hamilton

ISBN: 0-671-64750-4

First Minstrel Books Printing June 1990

10 9 8 7 6 5 4 3

Contents

Chapter One

Kiss of the Bag Lady

I tried to resist. I really did. But when I got the note saying, "This summer it's dinosaurs. Counting on you to be there!," I knew I had to go back to Camp Haunted Hills for another summer.

The note came from Harry Housen, the special-effects genius at Camp Haunted Hills, the camp where you learn to make movies. Special effects are what I want to do more than anything in the world. The thing is, at Camp Haunted Hills real life and special effects seem to get mixed up. At least, they do for me.

My very first night there I met a ghost named Robert, who had decided I needed his help because I was "the weirdest kid in the camp." Thanks to Robert's "help" I was kidnapped by a sasquatch, chased by a mummy, and menaced by a roomful of monsters.

Even so, saying goodbye to Robert when that first summer ended was tough. We had been through a lot together, and I was worried that he might be lonely.

"Me?" cried Robert. "Lonely? Stuart, people are dying to spend time with me!"

He floated away, laughing at his own joke. But when the bus pulled out of the camp parking lot that last day, I saw Robert sitting on top of a pine tree, watching us go. He might not have been lonely, but his expression wasn't what I would call happy.

Robert had been on my mind all winter. The only person I could talk to about him was Brenda Connors. That was because during the whole summer Robert had never let anyone other than me and Brenda see him, which was a little annoying, Brenda being a girl and all. Fortunately, she lives in another city, so I didn't have to cope with her too much that winter. Even so, it was good to have someone else who knew about Robert.

After I got Harry's note, I decided to give Brenda a call.

"So, are you going back to camp this summer?" I asked.

"Of course!" she said. Then, sounding a little worried, she asked, "Aren't you?"

"Sure," I said. "I'm going back."

"Well, I've got good news for you. Lucius isn't."

That wasn't just good news. It was like the government deciding chocolate should be free! Lucius Colton, creep *extraordinaire*, bane of my existence, wasn't coming back. I can cope with a ghost any day—just keep Lucius away from me.

That night I told my parents I wanted to go back to Camp Haunted Hills.

"Oh, honey," said my mother. "I don't know. You had kind of a rough summer last year."

"It was good for him!" said my father, who thinks I need toughening up. Of course, he didn't know more than half of what had happened to me at Camp Haunted Hills. But with him on my side, it didn't take much to talk my mom into it.

So the first week of July, there I was at the bus pick-up point, ready to go back to camp. Which probably proves that I'm out of my mind.

I discovered that the second time you go to a camp is a lot easier than the first time. The first time, you can feel lonelier than a minnow in the desert. You don't know anyone; even worse, you don't know the rules. The second time you know what to expect, how to act—you feel safe.

Part of that safety comes from meeting people

3

you already know. So I was actually glad to see Brenda. She had her light brown hair pulled back in a ponytail, and I noticed she had lost a little weight since the previous summer. I decided not to say anything. I didn't know how sensitive she might be about having been heavier the year before.

To Brenda's left and a step behind her stood a short, pudgy kid whose pale-blond hair had been cut very short. Brenda reached back and pulled the kid up beside her. "This is him," she said, pointing at me.

The kid looked as if he had just been introduced to a movie star.

"Are you really Stuart Glassman?" he asked in awe.

I looked at Brenda. What was going on?

"Stuart, this is my cousin, Winston de Pew."

I almost said, "Gee, I'm sorry about your name." But I stopped myself and took his hand, which he had put out for me to shake.

"You're my hero," said Winston as he pumped my arm up and down.

I blinked. No one—but no one—has ever considered me hero material. I'm skinny. My nose is a couple of sizes too large for my face, and I wear thick glasses. Indiana Jones I am not.

"Brenda told me about your adventures last

4

summer," continued Winston. "I hope something like that will happen to me this year."

I didn't figure it would do much good to tell Winston that adventures are better when they happen to other people. Personally, I was hoping that nothing even resembling the summer before would happen that year.

I might as well have hoped it would rain maple syrup.

Before Winston could say anything more, I saw the person I had really been looking for. "Harry!" I cried. "Harry, over here!"

Harry Housen, tall and gawky, with a nose even bigger than mine, had just wandered into the parking lot. His pet iguana, Myron, was riding on his shoulder. Harry looked really glad to see me. (I think Myron did, too, but it's hard to tell with an iguana.)

"Where's Aurora?" asked Brenda.

Aurora Jackson was the Camp Haunted Hills makeup expert. She and Brenda had gotten to be friends the summer before, in about the same way that Harry and I had.

Before Harry could answer, I saw another familiar face: Flash Milligan, the camp's lighting expert. Flash *does* look like a hero. He's tall and lean, with curly dark hair, broad shoulders, and a face like a Greek god.

Unfortunately, he's also a creep.

It didn't take him long to demonstrate that fact. An old bag lady came tottering across the parking lot. When she stopped and asked Flash for a handout he looked at her as if she were slime mold.

"Get out of here before I call the cops," he said.

The old lady spat on the ground. Then she hobbled over to Harry. "Got any spare change, mister?" she whined.

I drew back a little. The old lady really was disgusting. She had gray, stringy hair and a big wart on the end of her chin. One of her eyes was swollen shut, as if it had some kind of infection.

Harry dug in his pocket and hauled out a couple of quarters. "Here you go," he said kindly.

"Thanks, mister," said the bag lady.

Then she reached up, grabbed Harry by the ears, and kissed him on the lips.

Chapter Two

Winnie the Wimp

People started to hoot and cheer. Harry struggled and tried to pull away.

"Look!" cried Winston, when the bag lady finally let go. "Oh, look!"

The bag lady's long nose was dangling from Harry's cheek. "You need to read your fairy tales, buster," she said, turning to Flash. "You should always be nice to old ladies you meet along the road." Then she pulled off her wig. A flood of sun-yellow hair tumbled down her back.

"Aurora!" cried Brenda. She ran up and threw her arms around the woman's waist.

"Just a second, hon," said Aurora. Unhitching Brenda's arms, she stripped off her bag-lady outfit. Underneath she had on jeans and a Camp Haunted Hills T-shirt. By the time she was done wiping the makeup off her face, Aurora looked

better than most of the women you see on magazine covers.

Flash put on his mirrored sunglasses to hide how mad he was.

"Hope I didn't startle you too much, sweetie," said Aurora, taking Harry by the arm. Myron crawled from Harry's shoulder to Aurora's.

Wow, I thought, *this must be serious*. I was glad. I thought Aurora and Harry made a good pair.

Flash didn't agree. He could never understand why Aurora would go for a guy who looked like Harry when she could have had his own gorgeous self instead.

Personally, I found it very encouraging. If I ever decide I want a girlfriend, it's nice to know I don't have to look like Flash to get a girl who looks like Aurora. Of course, that means *I* shouldn't care what *she* looks like either—which makes the whole thing too confusing to think about right now.

We climbed into the buses and began the long trip to Camp Haunted Hills in Oregon. My favorite part is when the bus drives over a cliff, and you think you're going to fall a couple of thousand feet and die. That's a great example of how the staff practices their special-effects skills.

Unfortunately, some people can't cope with surprises. When we started over the cliff, Winston let out a scream that nearly broke my eardrums.

"Didn't you warn him?" I asked Brenda after everyone had quieted down a little.

"I told him," she said. "But things like that bother him. At school they call him Winnie the Wimp."

She stopped, realizing her horrible mistake.

But it was too late.

"Did you guys hear that?" screamed Keith Carter. "His name is *Winnie the Wimp*!"

The news traveled from one end of the bus to the other almost instantly. Within seconds the traditional singing of "Ninety-nine Bottles of Beer on the Wall" had been replaced by several rousing choruses of "Winnie the Wimp," sung to the tune of "Winnie the Pooh."

Winnie's face turned bright red, and I could see he was fighting to hold back tears. "It'll be all right," I whispered. "They'll lay off in a few days."

When we finally got to camp, Winnie was pleased to find out that we were going to be staying in the same cabin, Bunk Thirteen. As for me, I was pleased to find out we had the same counselor as last year, Dan Snopes. Dan can imitate all kinds of people. Sometimes before lights out he would do comedy routines that had us falling out of our beds.

As we were walking to our cabin we saw an enormous snake slithering down a nearby tree. Winston's eyes got wider and wider as the snake sped toward us. Suddenly it reared up. Winnie shrieked in fright.

"Hi, kids," hissed the snake. "Anybody want an apple?"

Everyone except Winston started to laugh and cheer.

"I thought I was going to wet my pants," he whispered as we continued toward the cabin.

By the time we made it past mysterious mists, bloodcurdling screams, and other little welcomes the staff had prepared, Winnie was twitching like a rabbit's nose. It made me nervous just to watch him, and I was pretty twitchy myself by the time we got to the cabin.

"Okay, guys," yelled Dan, "into your swimsuits! Swimming tests in fifteen minutes!"

That was good news. I'm not much of a jock—I can't catch a ball to save my life—but I *am* a good swimmer. I grabbed my trunks and got ready to change.

"Here?" whined Winston. "We're supposed to change right *here*, in front of everyone?"

11

I started to snap at him. Then I remembered how I had felt the first time we had to change the year before.

"Hey," I said, "at least it's not the girls' cabin."

He turned red. It was clear my humor hadn't worked. Well, there was nothing else I could do for him. I guess learning to drop your drawers in front of other people is something a guy has to work out on his own.

As we were walking down to Misty Lake, Winnie pointed at a bird. "Look," he said. "There's a dinosaur."

"Gee, and you looked like such a smart kid," I said.

"I'm serious," said Winston. "Some scientists think dinosaurs didn't die off after all. Some might have evolved into birds. His ancestor might have been a Tyrannosaurus rex."

I was still laughing when we got back to the bunk. Then Winnie showed me a book that had the dinosaur-to-bird theory in it. That bothered me a little. I had thought I knew a lot about dinosaurs, but it seemed that Winnie knew more.

"I could have told you that," said a voice behind me.

I spun around. "Robert!" I cried.

"None other," he said happily.

"What are you looking at, Stuart?" asked Winston.

I paused. I knew Winston couldn't see Robert. So if I said I was talking to someone, he would think I was nuts.

"Oh, nothing," I said casually.

"Nothing!" cried Robert, floating over to stand between me and Winnie. "I like that! Haven't seen the guy for ten months, and he starts out by insulting me."

"Cut it out," I hissed between clenched teeth.

"I'm sorry," whimpered Winnie. "I don't know what I did, but I won't do it again. Don't be mad at me, Stuart. Just tell me what I did, and I promise I won't do it again."

"Ooh," said Robert. "Fragile little thing, isn't he?"

"I'll talk to you about it later," I said, managing to answer them both at once.

Feeling fairly smug about that, I went back to my bunk to unpack.

"I see your taste in underwear hasn't improved," said Robert, who was now hovering near my shoulder.

My answer was interrupted by a pounding at the door. Before anyone could get there, the door flew open by itself. Standing in the entrance was

13

a shaggy, seven-foot-tall creature—a sasquatch, just like the one that had kidnapped me the previous summer.

"I want Stuart Glassman!" it roared.

14

Chapter Three

Betsy the Behemoth

Winston screamed, jumped onto the top bunk, and shoved his head under a pillow. Some of the other guys shrank back against the sides of the cabin.

But I recognized the voice. It belonged to Harry Housen. The sasquatch was just a holographic messenger, telling me Harry wanted me to come to the special-effects shop (or the SFX lab, as we liked to call it). As soon as it had delivered the message, it faded out of sight.

I hotfooted it over to Harry's lab, which is about my favorite place in the whole camp, if not the whole world. I found him standing at one of the long tables, gluing a fin onto Myron's back.

"Stuart!" he cried. "I didn't expect you so quickly. I'm going to need your help for a big announcement tonight."

"Can I help, too?" asked Robert.

I rolled my eyes at him.

"Are you all right?" asked Harry.

"What? Oh, sure," I said. "So tell me, does this announcement have to do with dinosaurs?"

"Does it ever," Harry chuckled. "Wait till you see what I've been working on for the past six months."

He led me to the back of the special-effects shop. We stopped in front of a black door held shut by an enormous padlock. Painted on the door in big red letters were the words *KEEP OUT! TOP SECRET!*

As far as I know, I'm the only camper who has ever been allowed past that door. On the other side was Harry's private workshop. It was like special-effects heaven, filled with everything from high-tech cameras to buckets of fake blood.

Harry paused at the door. "We'll make most of our film with miniatures and with holograms. But you can only do so much with those things. To take the last step, we need . . ."

He paused, waiting for me to fill in the blank. I

16

thought furiously. Then it hit me. "A life-size, working model?"

Harry smiled and unlocked the door. "Behold," he said. "Betsy the Behemoth!"

He swung open the door. I stepped into the shop and found myself face to face with a life-size triceratops that stretched nearly the full length of the room.

"Cut my hair and call me baldy!" cried Robert. "That's amazing!"

I ignored him. "How big is she?" I whispered.

"Twenty-five feet long and nine feet tall," beamed Harry.

I reached toward the crest that curved back over Betsy's neck. The top of it was nearly a meter beyond my fingertips. I ran my hands over her pebbly skin. She looked so real I felt as if I had slipped back in time.

"Well, I am seriously impressed," said Robert. He was floating above Betsy's long upper horns. "She looks just like the real thing. Which reminds me, I haven't talked to a dinosaur in a while."

I scowled at Robert, trying to get him to shut up for a bit. "Something wrong?" asked Harry, when he saw my face.

"No!" I said, faster than necessary. "I was just

squinting to get a better look at some of the details."

Harry looked puzzled. But he was so odd himself that he was willing to forgive the strange things I sometimes did.

"I'm planning to unveil her after dinner tonight," he said, leaning against Betsy's enormous thigh. "I'd like you to ride her for me."

"What?"

"I want you to ride her into the dining hall to announce our project."

Harry liked to announce his projects in a big way—like the time he pretended to turn himself into a monster. That was for a film called *Dr. Jekyll's Nephew*.

I understood why he wanted to do it that night. Gregory Stevens, the man who created Camp Haunted Hills, likes to have the first supper of the summer be a special event. (Mr. Stevens's idea of special can be seen in his films, like the famous *Battle for the Galaxy* trilogy.)

I couldn't pronounce the names of half the food they served that night. Most of us had learned early on not to ask what went into the stuff we were eating. We'd discovered that a lot of fancy food tastes better if you don't think about it too much.

18

Unfortunately Winston didn't know that the rest of us wanted to stay ignorant. "Mmm," he said as we started our appetizers. "This is the finest *fwah gra* I've had in some months." (I checked on the spelling later; it's really *foie gras*. No wonder none of us could pronounce it.)

"You've had this stuff before?" asked Eddie "Freckles" Mayhew. He sounded astonished. But then, Eddie always has a hard time with the fancy meals. He's much happier when we get hamburgers and hot dogs.

"My parents serve it frequently," said Winston. "It's goose liver."

Eddie fell off his chair and lay on the floor, gagging.

"This kid is going to need a lot of help," said Robert, who had appeared in the air above Winston.

I had a little time after we ate before I had to do my bit. We were going to see a short film with a speech from Gregory Stevens. I wanted to watch because his new movie, *Temple of the Golden Arches*, was scheduled to open the next week, and I was hoping we might get some previews.

After the film they'd start staff introductions. That was when I was supposed to make my entrance on Betsy.

Halfway through the film I excused myself. I

stood by the door until the film was over, then slipped outside. (There were no previews, which was no surprise. Gregory Stevens is the most secretive man in Hollywood).

"Over here," hissed Harry. "Behind these trees."

Seeing Betsy out in the open was a shock. She looked more real than ever.

"You can climb one of the trees to get on," said Harry.

I scooted up a maple, then dropped onto Betsy's back.

"You look like a real cowboy," said Robert.

"I don't feel like one," I whispered nervously.

Still, it was going to be easier to ride Betsy than I had expected. Harry had made a kind of natural saddle behind her upper horns. You couldn't see it until you sat down. Then you realized that things were curved to help hold you in place. In front of each horn I found a little dent where I could rest my feet.

"I'll use this to control Betsy's movements," said Harry, holding up a black box covered with knobs and switches. "You can override the controls if you have to. Pull the left horn to turn left, the right horn to turn right. Did you find the footrests?"

I nodded.

20

"Good. Press your right foot to go faster, your left foot to stop."

"Where's the seat belt?" asked Robert. It was the most intelligent thing he had said all day. But before I could repeat the question to Harry, Betsy lurched into motion.

"*Yee-hah!*" whooped Robert, as Betsy began thundering toward the building.

I wondered if somebody would open the mess-hall doors. No one did. When we reached the building Betsy lifted her head, smashed open the doors, and hurtled right through.

The reaction was spectacular. Even kids who had been at camp before weren't expecting anything like Betsy. People were screaming. Some jumped onto their chairs (don't ask me what good that did). Others crowded against the far wall.

The camp director, Peter Flinches, had been making a speech. The look of total astonishment on his face when we broke through the door was great. However, I couldn't tell if it was real or not, since during the rest of the year Peter was a professional actor.

Betsy stopped in the middle of the room. The lights went out. Then a spotlight flared on.

"Ladies and gentlemen," said a deep voice, "this summer Camp Haunted Hills will attempt to make a film of stunning depth and realism. It will be called *The Day of the Dinosaur*. We want you to meet the star of that film, the world's only full-size, fully functioning robot triceratops—Betsy the Behemoth!"

Betsy reared up on her hind legs. The dining hall broke into wild applause.

It felt great—until Betsy went berserk.

Chapter Four

Ride 'em, Dinoboy!

I'll never forget the look on Harry's face when Betsy turned and charged right at him. If I could have seen the look on my own face, I probably wouldn't forget that, either. According to Robert, it was hilarious.

I might even have laughed about it later. At that moment, I was too busy worrying that I was about to become the world's first hit-and-run triceratops driver.

For about three seconds Harry twirled and twiddled the knobs on his control box. Then he tucked it under his arm and ran for all he was worth.

People screamed with laughter. The dining hall erupted with clapping and cheering. After all, it *was* Camp Haunted Hills. Everyone figured Betsy and I were just part of the show. For a moment, even I wondered if that might be the case. After all, Harry *had* kept that kind of secret from me in the past.

But Harry was a techie, not an actor. The terror on his face was too real for him to be faking it.

Harry raced through the door. The runaway triceratops thundered after him, with me bouncing up and down on top of it like popcorn in a popper.

"Use the brakes!" cried Robert, who was still floating beside me.

I pounded my foot on the brake. Instead of stopping, Betsy began to buck.

I grabbed her horns and hung on for dear life.

I heard cheering behind me and realized the rest of the campers had followed us out of the dining hall. "Ride 'em, Stuart!" they cried. "Ride that dinosaur!"

Harry began to run in a big circle. Betsy stopped bucking and followed him. When Harry tripped and fell in a puddle right in front of Aurora, I was afraid I would run right over both of them. But mysteriously, Betsy stopped.

My hands were trembling as I climbed over Betsy's horns. "Are you all right?" I cried, running to Harry.

He sat in the puddle, looking miserable. Mud dripped from his elbows, his nose, and his hair.

"I don't get it," he said. "What happened?"

Before we could try to figure it out, we were interrupted by Winnie. "Stuart, you were wonderful!" he cried, pushing his way through the crowd. He looked so excited and happy, I was afraid he was going to hug me.

Aurora held out a hand to help Harry to his feet. "You are truly an interesting person," she said, gazing at him with an expression that Harry later told me should be called "bemused affection."

Harry groaned. "I don't know what went wrong," he said miserably.

But Brenda knew what had happened. "It was Flash," she said as the two of us walked to the campfire circle later that evening. "He made another control box, and overrode Harry's control of the dinosaur."

"How do you know?" I asked.

"Robert told me. He saw Flash using it."

"*Robert* told you?"

I probably sounded a little foolish. After all, Robert had revealed himself to Brenda the previous summer, so there was no reason for him not to speak to her. I just hadn't been expecting it. To tell you the truth, I think I was a little jealous. I mean, Robert was supposed to be *my* friend.

26

Sounds stupid, I know. But that's the way emotions are.

I tried to calm down so I could think about what Brenda had told me. "I don't get it," I said after a while. "Flash couldn't invent something like that."

"He couldn't invent something like Betsy. But he's good enough at electronics to make a *copy* of the control box."

"But when? How? You know how secretive Harry is."

Brenda shrugged. "Harry was working on Betsy back in Hollywood for the last six months. Maybe Flash did something then. I know he was mad all winter because Aurora doesn't think he's any more appealing than dog drool."

I remembered the look Flash had shot me when I laughed at Aurora's trick at the bus station. He was someone who believed in getting even.

Great, I thought. Lucius was gone, but we were going to have to spend the summer dealing with a grown-up version of the same personality. The only real difference between them was that Flash was older and sneakier.

"You know, I never did like that guy very much," said Robert, popping into sight as Brenda and I settled down to watch the campfire.

27

"Well, for heaven's sake, don't do anything about it," I said. "If you try to get back at him, he'll only cause more trouble."

Robert suddenly looked alarmed. "Oops!" he said.

One good thing about having Brenda know about Robert is that sometimes I can talk to him by pretending to talk to her. The conversation may not always make sense, but at least people watching don't think I'm totally loopy. Looking at Brenda I said, "What have you done now?"

"Nothing much," replied Robert cheerfully. "I just had a little chat with some of my friends. Don't worry so much, Stuart, you'll give yourself wrinkles. This is going to be fun. Trust me."

When Robert says, "Trust me," it's time for a nervous breakdown. I prepared myself for whatever might happen next.

Of course, at Camp Haunted Hills it's hard to know what to look for in a situation like that. Every time something unusual happened that night, I wondered if it was the beginning of a disaster. A meteor fell from the sky to light the fire. Pink elephants danced behind Peter Flinches while he led the first song. A tree got up and walked across the clearing.

Each time I wondered, *Is this Robert's work, or just special effects*? But since none of them had anything to do with Flash, I decided they also had nothing to do with Robert.

Then Flash got up to lead a song. I knew from a conversation I had overheard the year before that he hated doing it. But it was a camp rule: all the staff had to take turns at helping with the entertainment.

Flash being Flash, he wasn't about to show that he was embarrassed. But he wasn't about to miss a chance to bug Harry, either. He announced we were going to sing a song about a dog, only we were going to substitute Harry's name for the dog's.

He tried to make it sound like good-natured teasing, but I thought it was one of the nastiest stunts I had ever seen. I started muttering under my breath. "Why that low-down, slimy, good-for-nothing . . ."

Robert heard me.

"Oh, good," he said. "Since you feel that way, you won't mind what's coming!"

29

Chapter Five

Robert's Revenge-
Part I and Part II

I was trying to figure out just what Robert had in mind when I felt something crawl over my hand. I looked down and saw a spotted salamander—a big one, about eight inches long. Another one was skittering along behind it.

"What's going on?" hissed Brenda, pulling her hand away from a long brown lizard.

I could hear rustling noises all around us now, even above the singing. But then, the singing wasn't quite as loud as usual, since people seemed a little uneasy about Flash's "joke" of using Harry's name.

"Robert?" I said nervously.

He put his fingers to his lips. "Shh," he said with a smile. "Just watch!"

Halfway into the second chorus, Flash got a funny look on his face. He started to shake one leg.

Then he started to shake the other.

He stopped singing and started to slap at his pants.

Everyone stared at him, wondering what was going on.

"It's the lizard army!" chortled Robert. Finally I realized what was happening: Robert had talked all the lizards in the forest into crawling up Flash's pants.

Flash was going nuts. "Get them off me!" he screamed, dancing around and tugging at his pants. "Get them off me!"

Finally he got his belt unbuckled. Tearing off his pants, he sent lizards and salamanders flying in all directions.

"Oh, yuck!" screamed the campers down front.

Robert was laughing so hard he was rolling around in the air. "Isn't this great?" he cried. "Just what that jerk deserves!"

Flash ran into the darkness, flailing at the little creatures crawling all over him and screaming, "Get them off, get them off!" He made Winnie the Wimp look like a hero. (Though to be fair, I'm not sure how I would cope with a batch of lizards crawling all over me.)

Of course, no one knew exactly what had happened. But Flash figured it was all Harry's fault.

He said so the next morning, just after breakfast.

"I don't know how you did that last night, Housen, but I'm not going to forget it."

"I didn't do anything," said Harry.

"Of course he didn't," said Robert smugly. "I did!"

It was a nice confession. Unfortunately, only Brenda and I could hear it.

"Oh, yeah?" said Flash to Harry. "I suppose you're going to tell me you didn't sic those lizards on me to get back for—" He stopped. No one had ever accused him of sabotaging Harry's dinosaur demonstration. Brenda and I knew what had happened, because of Robert, but no one else had the inside story. Flash had nearly given himself away.

"Get you back for what?" asked Aurora, who was standing beside Harry.

"Nothing," muttered Flash, his cheeks growing red. He turned back to Harry. "I'm warning you— mess with me again and I'll show you a whole new kind of special effects."

Poor Harry. Brilliant as he was, he just didn't understand people. The thought of a new special effect was too much for him. "Like what?" he asked eagerly.

"Let's just say I'll make you see stars in broad

daylight," said Flash. He wheeled and stomped away.

"What did he mean?" asked Harry.

"Jefferson Davis and my Aunt Mavis!" cried Robert. "That boy is slower than a peanut-butter river."

"What did he mean?" repeated Harry, who couldn't hear Robert.

"He means he'll hit you in the head," said Aurora.

Harry almost fell down. "I don't want him to hit me!" he said. The poor guy was terrified—which was just what you'd expect from someone Robert had decided to help.

That was the beginning of the war between Harry and Flash—or, more accurately, Flash's war against Harry and his movie.

It's amazing how much can go wrong when you're trying to make a film—especially when the lighting man has it in for you. I had already learned that when you're making a movie you spend at least half your time waiting for people to get stuff set up. If the guy setting stuff up wants to take his time, things can get real slow, real fast.

Things got slow for Harry's movie. And it wasn't just because Flash was dragging his feet. He was also sabotaging stuff. I know he was, because Robert told me.

The thing was, Flash was careful about it. He knew that if he got caught, it would mean his job. He also knew that if he was fired by Gregory Stevens, it would be a long time before he got the kind of job he liked again. The fact that he kept at it shows how much he hated Harry.

Harry wasn't the only one having troubles. I thought Winnie was going to set a camp record for getting the most noogies in a single week. By the first Friday of camp both Harry and Winnie were totally miserable.

"We'll never get this movie made," Harry moaned as we walked back to the special-effects shack after lunch.

"Unless we do something about that jerk, Flash," said Robert, who was floating along behind us.

"What can we do?" I asked, answering both Robert and Harry.

Harry only shrugged, but Robert smiled and told me he had an idea. Then *I* was the one who was terrified—especially when that ghost disappeared for the next twenty-four hours.

"What do you suppose he's up to?" asked Brenda. "I don't know," I said. "But the longer he's gone, the more trouble he can get into. I don't like this."

We were filming a scene with dinosaur miniatures in the special-effects lab the day Robert returned. He showed up about midway through the session, grinning like the idiot he is. I took one look at him and felt my stomach turn over. Robert in a good mood is annoying. Robert in a great mood is a reason to get truly nervous.

We had twenty people involved in the filming session. We were doing stop-action animation with miniature dinosaurs on a tabletop landscape. We would move the dinosaurs a tiny bit, take a picture, move them a little more, take another picture, and so on. When the film was shown on a screen, the dinosaurs would look like they were moving. It was slow work, but except for the fact that Flash was making it even slower than necessary, I really liked it.

Winnie the Wimp was working right next to me, of course. I couldn't shake the kid. It's nice to have someone think you're wonderful, but it can get tiring after a while.

Brenda was working with us, too. I didn't mind that as much as I would have the summer before. Brenda is okay for a girl. And she was good at what we were doing.

The Dinosaur that Followed Me Home

The three of us were working with a pair of tiny triceratopses. We were adjusting one of them when Robert appeared in front of us. "All set," he said, rubbing his hands with glee. "Keep your eyes open. In just a minute Flash is going to take a little trip."

Winnie must have seen the look of horror that crossed my face. "What's wrong, Stuart?" he asked. "What are you looking at?"

Just then Harry announced it was time for everyone to take a break.

"Except you three," he said, pointing to me, Brenda, and Winnie. "I want a close-up of these two critters for the next scene. Flash, come here, would you?"

"No!" cried Robert frantically. "Don't get near him!"

"What are you babbling about?" I asked, pretending I was talking to Winnie. The poor guy looked really hurt.

"Go!" cried Robert as Flash came wandering up. "Scram!"

It was too late. Robert's surprise arrived at the same time as Flash—which meant that we all disappeared together.

Chapter Six

Dinosaur Daze

For an instant I thought I had gone blind. Or maybe crazy. I felt like I was being whirled around. Strange noises screamed past my head in the darkness.

Then I began to see things that didn't make any sense: trees shrinking and growing, fires in the sky, rivers of ice flowing to a frozen sea. The world seemed to whirl faster and faster.

Brenda reached for my hand. I didn't snatch it away. When things get that weird, it helps to have someone to hold on to.

Suddenly we stopped. Just stopped cold. We landed on the ground—not the floor, the *ground*—with a thump.

"Where are we?" whispered Brenda nervously.

"I don't think we're in Kansas anymore, Toto," I said.

Sometimes a wisecrack can make you feel braver. That one didn't work, though; I was still terrified.

My first thought was that we had been shrunk. The place where we had landed looked a lot like the tabletop diorama we had been using for our film. We were lying under a kind of palm tree. In the distance I could see a smoking volcano. I looked up, half expecting to see the ceiling of the special-effects shack. Instead I saw a huge, clear sky. An enormous pterosaur was circling to our left.

Robert shimmered into view beside me. "Oh, great," he said. "*We* weren't supposed to end up back here. Just Flash."

"You mean this is your fault?" I started to ask. I stopped. What was the point? Of course it was Robert's fault. How else could it have happened?

I heard a groan nearby. It was Winnie. He had landed in a thick bush covered with berries, and was trying to pull himself out of it.

"Where are we?" he asked as I helped him to his feet.

"I don't know," I said. "Anyway, I think the more important question might be, *when* are we?"

Winnie looked at me like I was out of my

40

mind. He glanced around. *"What's going on here?"* he screamed.

Then he really got upset.

I didn't blame him. If I hadn't already been in so many weird scrapes on account of Robert, I might have flipped my lid, too. Oh, I was plenty scared, but I wasn't convinced I was going to die. At least, not yet.

About then Harry came staggering around a cluster of giant ferns. "Flash was right," he moaned, clutching his skull. "I see stars. But what did I do? Why did he wallop me?"

"Flash didn't hit you," I said. "Not unless he managed to whack you while we were traveling."

Harry looked up. "Traveling?" he asked. He looked around. "What's going on here?"

"Time vortex," said Robert, though Harry couldn't hear him. "It was meant for Flash. How was I supposed to know you four would be standing next to him when it hit? Usually you stay as far away from him as possible."

"We've gone back in time!" cried Winston. He couldn't hear Robert either, but he had managed to figure out the situation on his own. "Great Einstein, *we've gone back in time!*"

"Shut up!" I yelled, meaning both Winston and Robert. "We've got to think."

"The first thing we have to do is find Flash," said Brenda.

"Give me a break," groaned Robert. "If you're lucky, he's been eaten by a dinosaur." Being dead, Robert doesn't have a real strong sense of the sanctity of human life.

"He's back there," said Harry. "Come on, I'll show you."

We followed Harry around a clump of bushes. Flash was lying on the ground, clutching his head and moaning. Next to him lay his sunglasses. They were broken.

"He's not going to like that," I said, pointing to the shattered shades.

"He's not going to like that, either," said Brenda, pointing to our left.

I turned and saw a huge Tyrannosaurus rex heading in our direction. It was a long way away, but it was moving fast and looking cranky.

"Run!" yelled Harry.

"Walk!" said Winston. "If we run, we'll catch his attention. If we walk, he may leave us alone."

I glanced around. The monster was moving fast, but it didn't look like it was heading toward us in particular. And once I started to pay attention, I saw other little dinosaurs around that it might consider more edible than us.

We dragged Flash to his feet and started walking. It wasn't easy. All of us wanted to run like crazy, but what Winston had said made sense.

"Doesn't a Tyrannosaurus rex eat just about anything it can see?" I asked, glancing back nervously.

"Depends on how hungry it is," said Winston. "Scientists aren't sure about their metabolism. It's a matter of—"

"Tell him to save the lecture," said Robert. "Bluto over there just decided you look like lunch after all."

I looked back. The creature had picked up its pace. It was obviously stalking us. Then it began to run.

"Move!" I cried.

Winston spun around. "Run!" he screamed.

The tyrannosaur was amazingly fast for something so big. Every time I looked over my shoulder, that huge, fanged mouth was getting closer.

Chapter Seven

Our Friendly Neighborhood Dinosaur

It wasn't easy for Harry and me to run while dragging Flash between us. More than once I thought we should just drop him and save our own skins.

Harry wouldn't hear of it, which I suppose means he's nicer than I am. *Too nice*, I thought when I heard the roar of the hungry meat-eater coming up behind us.

Being devoured by a dinosaur while trying to save a creep was not my idea of how I wanted to die. Fortunately, Brenda spotted a cave.

"Look!" she cried. "Maybe we can hide there."

It seemed like a good idea—assuming there wasn't something just as bad as what was behind us lurking inside. But we had no time to worry about that. We sprinted for the cave and dove in.

As we lay there, gasping and panting, I kept

expecting the tyrannosaur to come roaring up to the entrance.

Nothing happened.

After a few minutes I crawled over the rocky floor to the mouth of the cave. Moving cautiously, I poked my head out.

The monster was nowhere in sight.

"Looks like Bluto's gone," I called, using the name Robert had given the monster.

Flash groaned. "Where are we?" he asked, trying to sit up.

"You don't want to know," said Brenda.

I think she spoke up because she figured she was the only one in the group Flash wouldn't hit. Personally, I wasn't sure about that, but I figured she was safer than I was.

Flash groaned again and slumped back against the cave floor.

Before any of us could speak, something small and furry skittered over Flash's chest. With a scream, he jumped to his feet. I think he stood up too fast, because he went down as quickly as he came up.

"Was that another lizard?" he moaned.

"I don't think so," I said as I watched the thing run out of the cave. "It was hairy." I paused. For some reason, that didn't make any sense to me.

45

Flash didn't answer. He had passed out again.

"Help me straighten him out," said Harry, walking to where Flash lay.

"It'll take more than you can do to straighten out that jerk," said Robert, drifting down through the ceiling. He floated over to me and said, "Aren't you going to say thank you?"

I raised my eyebrows in a wordless question.

"For saving your skins," said Robert. "That big guy would still be outside waiting for you if I hadn't shown him where to get some juicier meat."

I shouldn't have been surprised that Robert could talk to dinosaurs. After all, one of the first things he had done after meeting me was convince Harry's iguana to hide in my bed. And it was only a few nights since he had sent that army of lizards up Flash's pants. I wanted to ask him about it, but I figured it wasn't a good time. Instead, I turned to Winnie and said, "The thing that ran out of here was hairy."

"So?"

"So I thought only mammals were hairy."

"That's true."

"Well, what's a mammal doing in *dinosaur* times?"

For a moment I thought I had something. *Maybe this is just a bad dream after all*, I thought.

But it wasn't.

"There were plenty of mammals back then," said Winnie. He wrinkled his pug nose. "Or should I say *now*?" he wondered aloud.

I looked around the cave nervously. "Are you telling me there might be a saber-toothed tiger back there?" I asked, motioning to the darkness that stretched behind us.

Winnie laughed. "We're in the Cretaceous Period, silly. The *big* mammals won't be around for millions of years yet."

"How come you know all this?" I asked.

"Dinosaurs are his hobby," said Brenda, tucking her sweater under Flash's head. "He's been studying them since he learned to read."

"Which happened when I was three," said Winnie.

"Do you know anything about time travel?" I asked.

Winston frowned. "Mostly that it's not a good idea."

"It doesn't take a genius to figure that out," growled Flash. "Ow, my head! Where are we, anyway?"

We told him. Naturally, he didn't believe us.

So we took him outside to see.

It's sad to see a grown man cry—especially one

who's spent his whole life trying to be cool. In that case it was also scary, since I knew if we ever got out of the Cretaceous alive, Flash would never forgive us for seeing him break down and blubber. For a moment I wondered if he might kill us to keep his tears secret. Then I decided that even Flash wasn't that rotten.

As it turned out, I was right. He wasn't *that* rotten.

Just close.

While we were standing outside the cave, a little dinosaur came trotting in our direction. (By little, I mean that it was only about five feet taller than me.)

"Get back!" cried Flash, diving into the cave.

Winnie didn't move. "It's only a maiasaurus," he said. "A young one, too. It won't hurt us; it's a plant-eater."

He pulled a branch off a nearby bush and held it out to the little dinosaur. "Come here, fella," he said. "Want a bite of this?"

To my astonishment, the dinosaur came. I started to chuckle. It was a goofy-looking thing. With its stubby toes and big front lip it looked like a cartoon dinosaur.

"Why isn't it afraid of you?" I asked.

"Why should it be?" replied Winnie. "I'm smaller than it is!"

"Yeah, but human beings—"

I stopped. How would this thing know that humans were mighty hunters who wiped out whole species? We wouldn't be around for another seventy million years or so!

"I'll have a little chat with it," said Robert. "It might come in handy later on."

Between them, Robert and Winston charmed that little guy into being our friend. (Of course, Winston didn't know he was being helped by a ghost.) It was so silly-looking that Winnie named it Dingbat. I thought that was rude. But as Robert pointed out, the dinosaur wouldn't care.

We decided to go back into the cave to get out of the sun. Dingbat crouched down and followed us. I thought Flash might freak out, but he just slid back against the wall and sat there muttering.

"What I don't understand," said Winnie, stroking Dingbat's dark-green scales, "is how we went back in time in the first place."

"Strange things happen at Camp Haunted Hills," said Harry with a shrug.

"That's for sure," I replied, glad that he seemed to be willing to leave it at that. I had been wondering what Brenda and I should say to the others. If we tried to tell them about Robert, they would think we were bonkers. Though why anyone who had just been thrown seventy million years into the past would have a hard time believing *anything* is beyond me. Since I knew Robert wouldn't be willing to show himself, it was easier to leave the whole thing in the "unsolved mystery" category.

At least, it was easier for them. As for me, I wanted some answers. So that night, after the others had gone to sleep, I slipped out of the cave.

Chapter Eight

Under Ancient Stars

It was strange to stand under a sky seventy million years older than the one I grew up with. When I first looked up I cried out in shock. I thought there was something wrong with the stars. They were so bright! Then I realized it was just that the air was clear in a way no one who lives in our time has ever seen.

I tried to find the constellations until I realized they didn't exist yet. After that, I just stood and stared.

"Beautiful, isn't it?" whispered Brenda.

I jumped a little. "What are you doing here?" I asked.

"Probably the same thing you are," she said. "I want some answers."

I nodded. It was time to call Robert. But I didn't do it right away. It was kind of nice, just standing there with Brenda and looking at a sky no human being had ever seen before.

A soft breeze whispered by us. The night sounds I was used to—crickets and frogs—were missing. Instead I could hear the snorts and bellows of distant dinosaurs.

Brenda stepped a little closer. I felt the earth move.

That was because a brontosaurus was walking past. Its head was so high it blocked out some of the stars.

I decided it was time to get down to business. "Robert!" I said, trying to sound commanding. "Get out here. We want to talk to you."

He shimmered into sight, looking like a kid who had been caught stealing cookies. "Isn't this cozy," he said, glancing first at me and then at Brenda.

"Can the cute stuff," I said sternly. "We've got some questions for you."

"Oh, good. I love games."

"You love mischief," said Brenda.

"I can't deny it," he said. "A little nonsense is the spice of life—or, in my case, death."

I sighed. "Robert, we need to know how you got us here."

"And more important," said Brenda, "how to get home."

52

"Trust a woman to go to the heart of the matter," said Robert. "Though I must say that your attitude hurts my feelings, especially since I've just been arranging that very matter. The next bus out leaves at noon tomorrow."

Something slithered along the ground behind us. I pulled Brenda a step forward to avoid it. "The next bus?" I asked.

"A figure of speech," said Robert. "You have to catch a time vortex that's going your way. I found one that will pass about five miles from here."

"What's a time vortex?"

"Think of it as a drain in the great bathtub of the universe."

"I beg your pardon?"

"Look, I didn't invent these things," he said. "I'm just trying to explain how they work. There's a lot of time, see, and sometimes it starts pushing up against itself, and needs someplace to go. So there are these vortex things, which are supposed to relieve some of the pressure. They kind of drain off the excess time."

"Are there a lot of these things?" I asked nervously.

"They're all over the place, if you know where to look for them. But don't worry. Most of the time they're like me; they can go right through you and except for a little chill you wouldn't even notice."

"You mean when I shiver, it's because a time vortex is going through me?" I asked. I didn't like the idea.

"Either that or a ghost," said Robert. "Or it could just mean you have a lousy nervous system."

"I don't get it," said Brenda. "If these vortex things are supposed to pass right through people, then what are we doing here?"

"You shouldn't ask a question when you already know the answer," said Robert with a frown.

"I want to hear it from your own lips," replied Brenda.

Robert sighed. "All right, I admit it. I arranged for a vortex to pick up someone who was still alive. It wasn't easy, either, but I wanted to teach Flash a lesson. Who could figure you four would be standing next to him?"

"Well, since you arranged that, why can't you rig it so tomorrow's vortex comes right here, instead of five miles away?" I asked.

Robert sighed and raised his arms to the starry sky in exasperation. In the distance we heard a strange cry, something that sounded like a foghorn in love.

"Some people want everything," said Robert.

"Look, there's only so much a ghost can do, and I can't do anything about this. The truth is, I called in a lot of favors with the big boys to move that first vortex. We've already broken rules that shouldn't even be bent. There's just no way I can get that thing to come any closer."

"Well, how are we supposed to talk the others into this five-mile hike?" asked Brenda.

"That's your problem," said Robert.

"Maybe *you* should talk them into it," I said, "since this is all your fault."

"Stuart!" he said in mock shock. "I'm not that kind of a ghost. You and Brenda are all the human contact I need."

"Well, we're going to be *dead* human contact if you don't help us get out of here."

"What's the big deal?" muttered Robert. "It happens to everyone sooner or later."

I looked at him sharply. "Did it make a difference to you whether you died sooner or later?" I asked.

For once I didn't get a smart-alecky answer. "It made a difference," he said. Then he disappeared.

"I think you offended him," said Brenda.

"Don't worry about it," I said. "He's just gone off to sulk because I made him be serious for a minute."

"I heard that!" said a voice from the air next to me.

"Robert," said Brenda sweetly. "I've got an idea."

He reappeared, but not quite. He hovered in front of us, looking a little blurry around the edges.

"What is it?"

"Can you really talk to dinosaurs?" she asked.

"Sure," he said, sharpening his edges a little. "Not that they hold up their end of the conversation."

"Then let's try this," she said.

After she had outlined her plan I looked at her in awe. "Brenda," I said, "you're brilliant!"

"Thank you," she replied, making a little curtsy.

"And what am I?" asked Robert. "Chopped liver?"

"*Fwah gra*," I said. "And since you're the guy who got us into this, the least you can do is help us out."

"All right," said Robert. "I'll try."

Chapter Nine

Whirled Enough, and Time

I'm not used to seeing dinosaurs before breakfast. So when Dingbat ran up and honked at me the next morning, I squawked in fright and jumped away.

My squawk startled Dingbat as much as he had startled me. He turned and ran into the bushes.

I heard a laugh, and saw Robert floating nearby. Since I was the first one out of the cave, he was the only one who had seen my little exchange with Dingbat.

The reason I was out first was that I had never gone to sleep. I had tried, but I kept staring into the darkness, wondering if Brenda's plan would really work. I wanted to go home!

Dingbat came back, timidly stretching his neck toward me. He seemed friendly enough. When I reached out to scratch his chin he lifted his head

57

in pleasure and began to make a little chittering noise.

"You like that, buddy?" asked Robert, floating over to the dinosaur's head.

Dingbat nodded.

"Is he saying yes?" I asked in astonishment.

"Close enough. Heads up—here come the others."

Winnie stumbled out of the cave, rubbing his pudgy face. "I'm hungry," he said crossly.

Flash came next. I noticed that his normally perfect hair was tumbled into a messy mass of curls.

Harry followed, positioning his glasses on his beaky nose.

As soon as Brenda arrived, Robert put his head next to Dingbat's. I wondered if that was how they communicated. It seemed logical, since I knew they didn't do it with words.

A few seconds later Dingbat trotted away from the cave. He stopped, honked, then headed back toward us. When he reached us he honked again, then trotted away again.

"Hey," said Brenda, just as we had planned, "I think he wants us to follow him!"

"Don't be stupid," said Flash.

With Robert coaching, Dingbat repeated his performance.

"I think Brenda's right!" I said, trying to sound amazed.

"That doesn't make any sense," said Winston.

"Being here doesn't make any sense," I replied.

Dingbat ran through his routine a third time.

"See," said Brenda. "It's just like on 'Lassie'!"

"We might as well give it a try," said Harry. "What have we got to lose?"

"Our lives," muttered Flash.

But once the rest of us started walking, Flash came, too.

So far, so good. We had everyone going in the right direction. How long we could keep that up, I had no idea.

"I'm starving," whined Winnie after about ten minutes.

I was, too, but I didn't see anything that looked safe to eat. We did pass the carcass of a dinosaur. I suppose if we really had been starving, we might have cut off some of the meat. But we weren't quite that hungry yet.

"This is ridiculous," said Flash after an hour. "That dinosaur isn't taking us anywhere. We've got to do something about getting out of here."

"Do you have any suggestions?" I asked. He scowled at me, but at least he shut up for a while.

Robert and Dingbat led us to a ridge. From the

top we could see a herd of grazing triceratopses. They were enormous, but peaceful. We paused to watch them. Robert began fretting about the delay, but I don't think I could have gotten the others to move even if I had wanted to. And I didn't particularly want to. I didn't think I would ever see anything like that again.

On the other hand, if we didn't get to that vortex thing on time, I might be seeing stuff like that for the rest of my life. I was just getting ready to try to get us moving when I heard a sound in the bushes beside us. I turned, and saw a little triceratops poke its head out from some ferns. It looked a lot like Betsy, except it was only a foot high.

I know dinosaurs have to start out as babies. Even so, that one was a real surprise. I always think of them as being so *big*. Seeing one that didn't even stand as high as my knee was totally strange.

I held out my hand. The little guy waddled over, snuffling curiously. It was cute.

Suddenly I heard a roar behind us. I turned.

"It's Bluto!" I screamed. "Run for your lives!"

We must have made an amazing parade: two little dinosaurs, five frantic humans, one ghost, and a big, hungry, mean-looking T. rex. Anyone

60

who saw it from the outside would have been very amused.

Very terrified would be a good description of how it felt from the inside.

We sprinted through the undergrowth. Insects with wings as long as my arms flew up in alarm. Dingbat and the baby triceratops were squeaking with fear. (Actually, so were the rest of us.)

"Keep going!" yelled Robert. "You're almost there. You're almost there!"

He sounded pretty frantic himself. That surprised me. Robert usually stays calm, no matter how bad things get.

I tripped over a rock. As Winnie and Brenda helped me to my feet, I glanced back. The tyrannosaur was almost upon us.

"Gnyah!" I cried, sounding like Curly of the Three Stooges. "Let's move!"

Fear does wonderful things for your body. It makes your glands send out this chemical called adrenaline that gives you short bursts of amazing strength. I think each of us must have used up a year's worth of adrenaline, because we ran so fast that within a few seconds we were striding along beside Dingbat.

Unfortunately, adrenaline doesn't last forever. Mine was running out, and I was thinking of

falling down, when Robert yelled, "This is it! We made it!"

I glanced up. Ahead of me a tall, thin section of the world began to waver and ripple. It made me think of the way things look when you stare at them through the rays of heat that rise from a road on a hot day.

Before I could say, "So that's what a time vortex looks like," we were swept into it.

Around and around we swirled. Again I saw the strange visions. But this time I also heard a weird howling, a sound like worlds breaking apart. And I saw eerie shadows, things that might be, couldn't be, never had been, never should be.

I can't describe them. I only knew that something about them felt wrong. *Terribly* wrong. By the time the vortex dropped us, I was shaking with fear.

We landed about fifty feet from the special-effects shack. That was great. But we still had one problem—we had brought three dinosaurs back with us.

I didn't mind Dingbat and the baby triceratops. But the fact that we had managed to bring home a Tyrannosaurus rex had me worried.

Chapter Ten

Winnie's Warning

We might have died then and there if the big dinosaur hadn't been a little groggy. But you know how it is—the bigger they are, the harder they fall. Bluto the Tyrannosaurus rex was not little, and he had landed pretty hard.

On the other hand, he was plenty tough. Who knew how quickly he might recover?

Whining nervously, Dingbat and the baby triceratops ran to Winnie. I felt sorry for the poor things. They looked as confused as I had felt the first day of seventh grade.

"Robert!" I shouted. "Come here!"

I didn't care who heard me. I figured if anyone asked about it later I would say I had been hysterical, which wouldn't be far from the truth.

"Now what do we do?" I asked, when he popped up next to me.

"I don't know!" he said. He sounded close to hysterics himself. "This wasn't supposed to happen. I think I'm going to get in big trouble."

I saw Bluto's hind leg began to twitch. "He's waking up!" I hissed. "We're *all* going to be in trouble if you don't do something!"

Robert disappeared. "I'll try talking to him," said his disembodied voice. An instant later I saw him floating beside Bluto's head. That was something I had noticed about Robert. When he's with me, he never seems to move very fast. But when he blinks out of sight, he can reappear somewhere else almost instantly.

While Robert was whispering sweet nothings into Bluto's ear, Eddie Mayhew and some of the other campers showed up. At any other summer camp, they probably would have been totally freaked out. Not here.

"Wow!" cried Eddie, walking up to Bluto and patting him on the leg. "That's great, Harry. I love the things you make."

Bluto roared. Eddie jumped back, and I could see Robert trying frantically to keep the dinosaur under control.

"This is going to be a great movie," said Keith Carter. "When do we get to work with these guys?"

Harry started to babble an answer. He wasn't making sense, but that didn't make any difference because he was interrupted by another roar from Bluto.

Then Harry rose to the occasion. "You kids had better scoot," he said. "I've got some kind of problem with the programming and I have to fix it fast."

Eddie and the others looked hesitant.

"It's *secret*!" said Harry.

Eddie nodded. One thing you learn early at Camp Haunted Hills is that the counselors will teach you plenty of stuff, but you had better respect their secrets.

"Come on, guys," he said. "Harry will fill us in later."

Robert popped up next to me as the gang started to leave.

"The big guy is mucho hungry," he said. "Fortunately for you, he doesn't insist on having people meat. He's curious about it, since he's never had any before. But he'll settle for anything, as long as it's meat. I'll try to keep him calm while you guys raid the dining hall. Then I've got to go see what I can do about this mess."

I don't know which was more amazing: a hundred-and-forty-million-year round trip through time, or Robert saying he was going to take responsibility for a situation.

But then, from the hints he had dropped, I had a feeling he was going to have to answer to some kind of head ghost for this particular mess.

I turned to Harry. "Meat!" I cried, as if it had been my own idea. "Harry, we've got to get some meat to stuff down Bluto's throat."

It didn't take any argument. Harry could see at once that what I said made sense.

But not enough sense. "The *first* thing you'd better do is tie him up," said Flash, thereby offering the only good suggestion I had ever heard from him.

Being at Camp Haunted Hills, it was easier to find stuff to tie up a dinosaur than you might have thought. We went to the special-effects shack and brought out about three hundred feet of heavy-duty cable.

Finding the cable was easy. Figuring out what to do with it was not. None of us had been trained as cowboys, and the best way to truss a T. rex was not something that immediately sprang to mind. We wanted to do it without hurting him. For most of us, that was just a natural reaction. Count on Flash to say we had to be careful because Bluto was "a valuable specimen."

"Look at those teeth," said Winnie as we worked.

"Yeah, they're like carving knives," said Flash. "Stop gawking and get busy with that cable!"

We ended up making several loops of cable around Bluto's chest, then running the other end around a nearby tree. The others were amazed that he held still for this. Brenda and I were the only ones who knew that it was only Robert whispering, "Meat, meat, they're going to bring meat," into his ear that kept the dinosaur from ripping us to shreds.

As soon as we were done, Harry headed off toward the dining hall. He came back in a camp truck packed with five hundred pounds of hamburger.

"I hope this works," he said. "I told them we were filming a horror scene and needed some raw meat. They made me charge it against the special-effects budget."

"That should keep him happy for a while," said Robert as Bluto began wolfing down the meat. "Got to go! See you later."

Before I could protest, he was gone, leaving us with the three dinosaurs. I suppose we should have considered ourselves lucky that only one of them was an enormous carnivore.

Of course, since some of the kids had already seen them, it wasn't long before most of the camp was wandering by to take a look at Harry's new "project." Dingbat and Twitta (which is what Winnie had named the baby triceratops) loved the attention.

"No surprise," said Winnie. "Dingbat has no reason to be aggressive with anything smaller than himself. And of course the baby is more open to new experiences than an older dinosaur would be."

"Sure," I said. "That makes sense. What I want to know is, what are we going to do about these things?"

"Then you know about the problem?" asked Winston.

"What problem?"

Winnie looked nervous. "You mean you don't know? I thought it was obvious. If we don't get these dinosaurs home soon, the whole world is in danger."

"How much danger?" asked Brenda.

Winnie's eyes were wide. "We're talking about the end of life as we know it."

Chapter Eleven

Reality Shift

I stared at Winnie as if he had just come in from another planet. Then I said something intelligent. If I remember correctly, it was, "Huh?"

"We could change the entire shape of reality," he whispered.

"Winston," said Brenda, "what are you talking about?"

Winnie looked exasperated. "Think about it. By taking those dinosaurs out of their own time, we've changed the past. And that could change the present."

"What difference could three dinosaurs make?" I snorted. "There were billions of them!"

"What difference do *you* make?" replied Winnie.

I shrugged. "Not much, probably." I felt embarrassed. I would rather believe I'm going to change the world. But I could tell it was a time to be as honest as possible.

Winnie rubbed his hands over his pale face. I could tell he was trying to figure out how to get the idea into our heads.

"Have you got a chessboard?" he asked at last.

"Winnie," said Brenda, "this is no time for games."

"I'm not playing games! I want to show you something."

"I've got a chessboard," I said.

"Then get it," commanded Winnie.

"This better be good," I muttered as I walked back to Bunk Thirteen. I didn't notice Dingbat following me until I had gone half the distance. *Oh, well*, I thought, *he won't harm anything*. I just hoped he wouldn't get a bellyache from eating plants that hadn't yet evolved when he was born.

Dingbat waited outside the bunk while I got the chessboard. When I came out, I looked at him standing there and thought, *Why not?* Returning to the cabin, I found my backpack. I put the chessboard in the pack and strapped it on. Then I went back to Dingbat and stroked his long neck.

He bent down and rested his head on my shoulder.

72

It looked like we were friends. Hoping he would still think so when I was sitting on top of him, I threw one leg over his back and climbed on. I figured I had already ridden a mechanical dinosaur. Why not a real one?

Dingbat squawked and started to run. I wrapped my arms around his neck and held on. It took only a few moments for him to calm down. By the time we made it back to the special-effects shack, he actually seemed to like the idea.

"Here's your chessboard," I said, sliding to the ground in front of a nearly speechless Winston.

He shook his head. "You shouldn't do things like that," he muttered. "We have to try not to do anything that might change them."

I started to protest. But before I could say anything Winnie opened the chessboard and said, "How many squares?"

I didn't need to count—I knew there were sixty-four.

"Right. Now, how important are pennies?"

"Not very. I know kids who throw them away because they don't like to bother with them."

"I heard the government is thinking about not even making them anymore," added Brenda.

"Okay," said Winnie. "So pennies are no big deal. Now let's say you put one penny on the first square of the board. Put two pennies on the second square, four pennies on the next, and eight pennies on the next. If you keep doubling the pennies like that, what do you think the board will be worth when you're done?"

I did some quick addition. The whole first row was worth less than three dollars. On the other hand, I figured this was some kind of trick question, so I guessed high.

"A few thousand dollars," I said, feeling smug.

Winnie was even smugger. "You're not even in the ballpark. The answer is over a hundred and eighty quadrillion dollars."

"Would you try that with zeros?" asked Brenda.

Winnie shrugged. Picking up a stick, he wrote the number on the ground: $180,000,000,000,000,-000.

"How much is that in real money?" I asked.

"I don't think there *is* that much real money," he said. "Not in the entire world. It would run the United States government for the next hundred thousand years—which is about ninety-three thousand years longer than there have been governments."

"That can't be right," said Brenda.

Winnie set out to prove it. When he hit $327.68 at the end of the second row I figured we were in trouble. When he showed us that the last square on the fourth row was worth over twenty million dollars all by itself, I knew he was telling the truth. Try it yourself if you don't believe me.

"I still don't see what this has to do with the dinosaurs," said Brenda.

Winnie dug in his pocket and held up a penny. "People call this small change," he said. "Well, let's say that it stands for a real change—a *small* change one of those dinosaurs might make. Moving a rock, for example. Now imagine that each small change creates another small change. Just a tiny change. Like, because the rock is in a new place, a plant doesn't grow there. Because the plant doesn't grow, a certain insect doesn't lay its eggs there. That kind of thing. Each change causes a couple more changes, each one of them tiny, no more important than this penny.

"But double the pennies from square to square, and in only sixty-four steps you go from one cent to more money than there is in the entire world."

He looked me in the eye. "Even if we talk about only one set of changes a year, when we took those dinosaurs out of their own time, we started a chain that has at least sixty-four *million* steps. We don't even have *names* for the kinds of numbers you would get in a chain like that. But I can tell you this: that's more than a million changes for every grain of sand in the world. So you tell me—how different do you think the world would be if we changed that many things?"

I swallowed, remembering the terrible howling I had heard as we came back through the time vortex. Were the weird images I had seen signs that reality was starting to change?

The world seemed to swim around me. How could I think I was unimportant, when anything I did might start a chain like that? Suddenly I understood that everything you do counts. Everything matters.

The idea scared me silly.

But Winnie wasn't done. "And imagine that one of those dinosaurs was going to cause a *big* change. Let's say Bluto was about to eat some small dinosaur that was unusually intelligent. Since he isn't there to eat it, maybe a race of intelligent dinosaurs will develop. Maybe humans will be nothing but their pets. Or maybe we won't exist at all. Or we'll be all scaly or something."

"But we're not," said Brenda.

Winston sighed in exasperation. "That might

76

be because the dinosaurs are still alive, which means there's a chance to get them back without changing the past. But what will happen if one of them dies? There might be a total reality shift. The scary thing is, we wouldn't even know about it."

"Why not?" I asked, though I wasn't sure I wanted to know.

"Because we would never have existed as we are now. If we turn out to be lizard people instead of human beings, we would have always been that way. So we wouldn't even know about the change."

I felt like the top of my head was going to come off.

"Are you kidding me?" I yelled.

"I wish he was," said Robert, who had showed up to listen to the end of the conversation. "But it's true. If we don't get those dinos out of here soon, you may find the universe shifting around your ears."

I grabbed my ears and stared at the ground, looking for some sign of the reality shift.

"Forget it," said Winston. "You won't even know it when it happens. One minute you'll be you— the next minute you'll be something else altogether. Or maybe you just won't exist. Of course, it won't just happen to you. We're talking about every human being on earth.''

I stared at him in horror. I don't like being responsible for the family dog, much less the fate of the world.

Chapter Twelve

Seeds of Doubt

For the next few hours I kept staring at the people around me, trying to catch them shifting into something else.

It was weird, though. Because nothing happened right away, I started to worry about everyday things again. I mean, I knew there was this terrible situation that could destroy the world, but after a while, I still wanted lunch. Maybe that's why we still have nuclear bombs.

Anyway, there wasn't much point to living in terror. The point was to do something about it.

But what? Robert was the only one who knew anything about the vortexes, and he was nowhere to be found. He had claimed he was going off to try to do something about the mess we were in, but that didn't make me feel very confident.

"The main thing right now," said Winnie,

"is to avoid doing anything that might change them."

We were sitting in Harry's workshop—Harry, Brenda, Winnie, and me. Winnie had Twitta in his lap and was feeding her apple slices. I noticed he was keeping the core far away from her snapping mouth.

"For example," he continued, almost as if he were reading my mind, "we can't let them eat any seeds."

Twitta stretched her neck forward and snatched another slice of apple from his hand.

"Why not?" I asked.

"Because if we do manage to get them back, we have to be sure they don't take any seeds with them. Apple trees growing in the Cretaceous could cause a major reality shift."

"Well, seeds they eat aren't going to *grow*," I said scornfully.

Winnie just gave me a look.

"Oh, right," I said, remembering an old science lesson about how birds spread plants by eating fruit and then pooping out the seeds, which can still sprout. Suddenly I understood why he was holding the apple core away from Twitta so carefully.

I shivered. The idea that the whole world could

be changed by a little dinosaur poop made life seem awfully fragile.

"I think our biggest worry is bacteria," said Harry, who had figured out the time problem on his own. "We don't want these guys to carry back some modern germ that could wipe out the entire dinosaur population."

Twitta chose that moment to sneeze. You can't imagine how cute a baby triceratops is when it sneezes. Even so, we all looked at her in horror.

"Is she coming down with something?" I demanded.

Winnie swallowed nervously. "Maybe it was just something in the air," he said, trying to sound hopeful.

A knock at the door made all four of us jump. "I'd better put up a Do Not Disturb sign," muttered Harry as he went to answer the door.

But it was Aurora, and I knew that as far as Harry was concerned she could disturb him any time of the day. (Actually, I think every male in the camp felt the same way.)

"Where have you four been?" she asked. "You missed supper."

"Uh . . . we've been having a conference," said Harry. "We're trying to figure out what to do about the dinosaurs."

81

Aurora frowned. "Why are you being so secretive, Harry? You never told me you were making three more of those things."

Her voice sounded really hurt. I could tell she felt left out.

"Uh-oh," whispered Brenda. "Harry's in trouble."

I figure I need to learn all I can about dealing with women, since I'll have to do it someday. So I watched to see what Harry would do.

He dithered for a few seconds, rubbing nervously at his big nose. I began to realize that he probably isn't the world's best role model when it comes to dealing with women.

But at least he was sincere. And that was the approach he finally decided on.

"I have to tell you something," he said. Taking Aurora by the hand, he led her to where the rest of us were sitting.

"This ought to be interesting," whispered Winnie, his pudgy face glowing in anticipation. He put Twitta on the floor. She wandered around a bit, then went over to sniff at Aurora's leg.

Harry pointed at Twitta. "That," he said, "is not a robot."

Aurora snorted. "Well, what is it?" she asked.

"A dinosaur."

From the set of her chin it was clear Aurora

didn't believe him. I didn't blame her. If I hadn't lived through that trip to the past, I wouldn't have believed him, either.

"I'm serious!" said Harry.

"She's getting mad now," Brenda whispered.

I nodded. I could see Aurora's face turning deep red.

"Kids!" said Harry desperately. "Tell her!"

We told her. She still looked skeptical. I think the only thing that kept her from walking out was the fact that she had lived through some pretty weird stuff herself the summer before.

"What do you want me to do?" asked Harry desperately. "Cut one of them, so you can see it bleed?"

"Don't do that!" cried Winston. "You might give it an infection!"

Winnie's reaction did the trick. His concern was so genuine that Aurora's disbelief started to waver.

"Show me the other ones," she said.

We took her out behind the shop. Dingbat was tied to a post in the middle of a well-mowed area. He was munching on some food that Winnie had gathered for him. I looked at the pile and realized that it was all leaves and branches—not a single thing with seeds.

Winnie may be a little weird, but I was suddenly glad we had him around.

"Hey, Dingbat!" yelled Harry.

Dingbat raised his head, but continued chewing, shifting the lump of food from one cheek to the other. He looked like some goofy dinosaur version of a ten-foot-high cow.

"See," said Harry. "He's eating! Robots don't eat."

"Robots do what they're built to do," said Aurora.

Harry blinked in dismay.

"She's just teasing him," whispered Brenda. "We've got her convinced."

I started to ask her how she knew, but I decided it was probably some womanly mystery, so I kept my mouth shut.

We walked on to where Bluto was tied. We didn't have to worry about *him* eating seeds. He was only interested in one thing. Meat.

He turned his enormous head and glared at us.

"See," said Harry, spreading his hands. "No control box."

"Okay," said Aurora. "I believe you. You're good, but you're not that good."

"What's that supposed to mean?" asked Harry, sounding offended.

Aurora laughed. "Don't worry about it, sweetie. I believe you, all right?"

She took his arm, and we took the hint. At least, Brenda got the idea. "Come on," she said, giving me a nudge with her elbow. "Let's go back and take care of Twitta."

"Twitta's fine," I said. "I want to—"

"I said, let's take care of Twitta!" said Brenda more fiercely. She rolled her eyes toward Harry and Aurora.

"Right," I said. "Let's take care of Twitta."

As it turned out this was a particularly good idea, since when we walked into the shop Twitta was squawking in terror.

Chapter Thirteen

Vortex Alert

It was Flash, of course. He had Twitta under one arm and he was trying to hold her beak shut with the other hand. She wriggled and snapped at him, and he almost dropped her.

"What are you doing?" yelled Winnie.

"None of your business, geek," snarled Flash.

Outrage overcame my normal caution. "Flash," I said, "put down that dinosaur."

He laughed. No surprise, since he outsized me by twelve inches and fifty pounds.

What *was* a surprise was Winnie. He put his head down and ran straight toward Flash. I could tell he was planning to ram Flash in the stomach.

Flash dropped Twitta, who squawked with dismay. Holding his hands in front of him, he caught Winnie by the head. Winnie squirmed and shouted. For a minute I was afraid Flash was going to start hitting him. But then I realized that even Flash wasn't that dumb. Hitting a camper would be more trouble than it was worth.

While Winnie was struggling with Flash, Brenda grabbed Twitta and made a run for it.

"Get back here!" bellowed Flash, flinging Winnie aside. He ran after Brenda. My foot happened to be in his path, and he hit the floor with a thud.

Great, I thought when I saw the look on his face. *I've survived monsters and dinosaurs, only to get beaten to death by a jerk.*

But Flash ignored me. Grabbing a videotape from a nearby table, he snarled, "You twinkies win for now. But it won't last long. This will be enough for what I want."

Then he slammed out the door and disappeared.

"What did he mean by that?" asked Winnie.

I shook my head. "I don't know. Maybe he took pictures of Twitta."

Winnie's eyes went wide. "What do you think he's going to do with them?"

I wasn't sure. Whatever it was, I figured it was (a) to Flash's benefit and (b) not good for the rest of the world.

Robert agreed. He showed up the next morning and when I filled him in on the situation he actually shuddered, which is a truly weird action when performed by a ghost.

"So have you found a way to get them back?" I asked.

"I'm trying!" said Robert. "You have no idea how I'm trying, Stuart. And skip the cheap joke about how trying I am. I've got my ectoplasmic butt in hot water up to my neck."

"That doesn't make any sense," said Brenda.

"The universe doesn't make sense!" snapped Robert. "Speaking of which, I've got to warn you about something."

That made me really nervous. If Robert bothers to warn you about something, you can bet it's a real problem.

"While I was gone I found out that after you've been in a time vortex, you stay sensitive to them for a while."

"What does that mean?" asked Brenda.

Robert looked embarrassed. "Basically that if you happen to run into one you'll get swept into the past again. Or maybe the future. It depends."

I looked at him in horror. "Are you serious?"

"Dead serious."

I ignored the pun. "How long will this last?" I asked.

"Another three or four days. When you can't

see them anymore, you'll know they can't pick you up."

"We'd better tell Harry and Winnie," said Brenda. "Flash, too, I suppose. But we're not going to be able to explain to them *how* we know about the vortexes."

"Maybe we should start with Winnie," I said. "Then he can tell the others. They might believe him. They'll figure it's some kind of thing they never learned about."

"So how do we explain it to Winnie? You know how he is. He'll want some sort of scientific explanation."

"Just because people don't know how a thing works doesn't mean it's against the rules of science," said Robert.

I looked at him. I turned to Brenda. She smiled.

We both turned back to Robert. "We just figured out who should explain this to Winnie," I said.

He put up his hands in dismay. "Oh, no. Two mortals is enough. I don't need someone else to talk to."

"Nonsense," I said. "You'll love it. Besides, think of how interesting it will be for you to explain this scientific idea, when the fact that you exist goes against all the science we know."

"I resent that," said Robert.

"I resent being snatched sixty-five million years into the past!" I snapped. "I resent finding out that someone pulled the plug on reality. I resent the idea that I may wake up as the family dog tomorrow and not even know it. And I resent being told that I might be sucked up by the nearest time vortex and deposited somewhen else altogether."

"Well, since you put it that way," said Robert. "Maybe I'll talk to him."

"We'd better be there," said Brenda. "This won't be pretty."

It wasn't. Winston de Pew wasn't called Winnie the Wimp for nothing. When Robert appeared to him, he acted as if he had just seen a ghost. I suppose that's reasonable. But he acted like someone seeing a ghost in a bad movie. His eyes bugged out. His shoulders hunched up and down. He didn't move for about thirty seconds—not because he wasn't trying, just because his body wouldn't do it. Then he screamed and dove under the nearest bush.

"I told you this was a bad idea," said Robert.

"Oh, shut up!" I said savagely. I went over to the bush to drag Winnie out.

"That wasn't very nice of you guys," he whimpered, as we pulled him to his feet. "I know you can do all kinds of special effects here. But I didn't think the two of you would try to scare me like this. Especially not you, Stuart."

"This is no special effect, Winnie," said Brenda gently.

I could feel Winston stiffen up. He dug his heels into the ground. "It is, too!" he screamed. "It has to be."

I shook my head. "No joke," I said softly. "Camp Haunted Hills honor."

"Oh, puh-leeze," moaned Robert.

"No," whispered Winston. "No, it isn't possible."

"Look, kid," said Robert, "I don't want to scare you. I just want to talk to you."

"*You* don't scare me," said Winston. "You're only a ghost."

The look on Robert's face made me laugh out loud. I'd never seen him so offended.

"Well, what are you so upset about?" asked Brenda.

"The fact that he exists at all," said Winston, plopping down on the ground and adjusting his glasses. "If he's real, then who knows what else might be real? If he's real, then the world doesn't make sense anymore."

"Never did, as far as I know," said Brenda.

" 'There are more things in heaven and earth, Horatio, than are dreamt of in your philosophy,' " said Robert. "That's from Shakespeare. I was talking to him a few months back."

"You know Shakespeare?" asked Winston in awe.

"Don't get him started," I said. "Whenever I mention anyone who's both famous and dead, Robert always claims he's one of that person's best friends."

"I'm good company," said Robert cheerfully.

"And I'm Queen Mary," I said.

"Are not. I've met her. She doesn't look a bit like you."

I threw up my hands in disgust. "Look, just tell Winnie about the time vortexes, will you?"

"I can do better than that," said Robert. "If he turns around, he can see one. On the other hand, it's heading right this way. So maybe you'd better run for your lives!"

I should just have taken his word for it. But you know me—I had to turn and look.

Chapter Fourteen

Flash Back

The vortex was racing toward us like a small tornado, weaving its way back and forth across the campgrounds. Wherever it passed, the world seemed to wrinkle and then fall back into shape behind it.

"Amazing!" said Winnie.

I didn't say a thing. I just grabbed his arm and started to run.

I hoped the thing would veer off in another direction. But every time I looked over my shoulder, I could see that it was still heading right at us.

My breath began to feel like fire in my lungs, but when I slowed down Robert yelled, "Stuart, it's getting closer!"

I pumped my legs harder than ever. But I'm a swimmer, not a runner. Finally I ran out of power and threw myself to the ground. I lay there, gasping for air, thinking the next face I saw might belong to Og the Caveman or Ka, the Queen of the Future.

But rather than snatching me up, the vortex veered off to the right. I peered around cautiously and saw Brenda nearby. When we were sure it was safe to move, we crawled to a nearby tree and sat up against it.

Winnie sagged down between me and Brenda. His face was red, his eyes round and bright. "What *was* that thing?" he gasped.

"That," said Robert, floating down from above us, "was a time vortex."

"That's neat!" said Winnie when Robert had finished his explanation.

"Neat," I said bitterly. "It's not bad enough we have to worry about reality shifting widdershins on us. Now we have to keep a lookout for wandering time vortexes."

"I thought you loved danger and adventure!" said Winston.

I looked at him as if he had just suggested that I love liver pie. Before I could straighten him out, Eddie Mayhew came running along the path. He was panting and puffing, and his face was so red I could barely see his freckles.

"There you are!" he yelled. "You'd better come quickly. Flash just showed up with a reporter from *People* magazine and a scientist from the Dinosaur Institute. They're demanding to see Harry's secret project."

"We can't let them do that," Winnie whispered to me. "If they realize the dinosaurs are real, they'll take them off to study. If that happens, we'll never get them back to their own time, and there's no telling what will happen to history then!"

"Not only that," said Robert. "I've finally got the return trip worked out. We need to have the dinosaurs at the cliff by the lake in an hour. That's the only vortex back for the next two weeks." He looked worried. "This isn't 'be there or be square.' It's be there or be totally rearranged!"

I nodded grimly. "Where's Harry?" I asked Eddie.

"At the main office. He's trying to convince Mr. Flinches not to let anyone see his project."

"I've got an idea," said Brenda. "Eddie, can you find Aurora? Ask her to meet us behind the special-effects shack."

Eddie nodded and ran off the way he had come.

"What do you want Aurora for?" I asked.

"We're going to disguise the dinosaurs," said Brenda.

95

"As what?" I asked. "Small mountains?"

"You'll see," she replied, smiling mysteriously. "Let's get moving."

We trotted back to the SFX shack, keeping a nervous eye out for stray time vortexes.

Dingbat and Twitta were glad to see us. Bluto just looked cranky. But then, I'm not sure a Tyrannosaurus rex has any other expression.

Before I could quiz Brenda about her plan, Aurora came running up. "Eddie told me you needed me," she said, pushing her golden hair into place. "What's the problem?"

We explained.

"What can we do about it?" she asked.

Brenda pointed to the dinosaurs. "Can you make these guys look fake? You know—like they were mechanical instead of real?"

I stared at Brenda with admiration.

Aurora smiled. "I can try," she said. "Go get one of my makeup kits, hon."

Brenda trotted into the SFX shack, where Aurora kept some extra supplies. When she returned with the kit, Aurora got to work painting bolts and screws on Dingbat.

"I won't make them look too fake," she said, "because then people might get suspicious. They

96

know how careful Harry is when he makes something."

When Aurora finished Dingbat she started on Twitta. The little dinosaur squirmed impatiently. But that was nothing compared to Bluto. When Aurora started to get near him he threw back his head and roared. Then he stretched his neck out and snapped his jaws, as if he wanted to eat her.

Aurora turned white. "You know, there's a major problem with this idea," she said. "If we try to claim these dinosaurs are all mechanical, people are going to want to know why we tied that one to a tree."

"No problemo," said Robert, suddenly appearing to Aurora's right.

Winnie, Brenda, and I all turned to look at him.

"Something wrong?" asked Aurora.

"I thought I heard trouble over there," I said, gesturing toward Robert.

"I like that," he said.

"Well, do you have any suggestions?" asked Brenda.

"Not me," said Aurora.

"I thought you'd never ask," said Robert. "Here's the plan. It's wonderfully simple. We just have Stuart sit on Bluto. When the people Flash brought back see that, they're bound to think these things are fake."

97

"You've got to be kidding!" I cried.

"I'm serious," said Aurora, sounding offended. "I don't have any ideas."

"It'll work," said Robert. "I'll sweet-talk him while you're on his back. Assuming he's been fed lately, you won't have a thing to worry about."

"I think you'd better do it, Stuart," said Winnie.

"Do what?" asked Aurora, sounding confused.

"Plan B," said Brenda quickly. "Stuart rides the dinosaur."

"You've got to be kidding!" said Aurora.

"We've already had this conversation," said Robert. "Climb on, Stuart."

I walked over to Bluto. He looked down at me, and I swear he grinned. He had teeth like daggers, and breath that reminded me of the way our refrigerator had smelled when we came home from a two-week vacation and found out that it had broken a week after we'd left.

Robert floated over and put his head against Bluto's. They were silent for a moment. Bluto lifted his head and roared. The noise was deafening, like a dozen bull elephants all trumpeting at once.

"He's ready," said Robert.

Swallowing hard, I threw my leg over Bluto's tail and started to climb his back.

Chapter Fifteen

Bluto to the Rescue

Bluto was close to twenty feet tall. His mouth was big enough to bite me off at the belt line. He had a look in his eye that would have made a junkyard dog look like it belonged on "Sesame Street."

Saying that I was nervous is like saying that getting run over by a truck is annoying. "Steady, boy," I whispered as I pulled myself over his smooth scales. "Steady."

"Stuart, what are you doing?" cried Aurora.

"Trust me," I called down to her. I swallowed. The ground was a long way down. I decided to focus on Bluto's back.

"Stuart, be careful!" said Brenda.

"Don't worry!" called Robert. "I'll take care of him."

"That's what I'm afraid of," I muttered.

The funny thing was, once I got a good grip on Bluto's neck, I felt fairly safe. Since I was on the back of his neck, he couldn't bite me. He was still tied up, and his tiny front legs were far too short to grab me. Heck, he couldn't even scratch his own chin!

"Way to go, Stuart!" cried Winston. His pudgy face was split by a huge grin.

The smile I gave him in return was pretty weak. I felt a little safer, but I sure didn't feel heroic. Still, I figured I could hang on long enough to convince the intruders that if Bluto was letting me ride him, he couldn't possibly be real.

Unfortunately, that was when the time vortex showed up again.

Brenda was the first to spot it. "Look!" she screamed. "Over to your right!"

I looked where she was pointing and saw that frightening ripple, like heat rising from a road, zigzagging its way toward us.

"That's the wrong one!" cried Robert. "If it picks up the dinosaurs, there's no telling where they'll end up. We've got to get them out of here. Winnie, untie Bluto. Stuart, hang on. You're going for a ride!"

"*All right!*" cried Winston. He ran to the back

of the tree to undo the cables that held Bluto in place.

"What are you doing?" cried Aurora.

"Saving the world!" announced Winston, his pudgy face glowing.

"Are you out of your mind?" cried Aurora, who couldn't see either the vortex or Robert. "This thing could eat half the camp."

She ran toward Winston to try to stop him. She was too late. All it took was a loosening of the cables and a whisper from Robert, and Bluto was lunging forward with all his strength.

Five seconds later he was free. It sure wasn't like riding Betsy or Dingbat. I was heading for the camp headquarters on a real Tyrannosaurus rex.

It occurred to me that Harry would be sorry he didn't have the whole episode on film.

"Having fun?" asked Robert, who had settled himself on top of Bluto's head.

"Loads!" I screamed, trying to keep from slipping down Bluto's back. The motion of his great hind legs pounding the ground nearly shook me off. That was scary. Confident as Robert seemed, I wasn't convinced he could talk the tyrannosaur out of eating me if I hit the ground.

"Let's have some sound effects," said Robert. He placed his head against Bluto's.

A second later a savage cry ripped through the air.

"That should let them know we're coming," said Robert.

He was right. By the time we reached the center of the camp dozens of kids had come running in to see what was going on. With Robert directing Bluto, we trotted past them, up the trail toward the main office.

When we arrived, Bluto let out another bellow. A group of campers came running up behind us, laughing and cheering.

The door of the office flew open. Flash ran onto the porch, clutching a tall, bearded man by the arm. Harry and Peter Flinches came crowding out after them, followed by two or three other people I didn't recognize.

"See!" said Flash. "See, I told you. A real dinosaur!"

The man looked totally confused. I knew what he must be thinking. Bluto certainly *looked* real. But if he was real, then why wasn't he munching out on Camper McNuggets?

I laughed like crazy. It came naturally, given the fact that I almost was crazy with fear. "Real?" I cried. "You've got to be kidding! This is a robot!"

Harry got the hint. "Does anyone here seriously think a Tyrannosaurus rex would let a kid ride on its back?" he asked.

The bearded man smiled a little. "This is a very nice piece of model making. If you ever decide you want to leave filmmaking, I think I can find a job for you at our museum."

Then he turned to Flash. "I appreciate your wish to bring attention to your friend's talent. However, I must protest this prank. I have far too much real work to spare any time for this kind of nonsense."

"Friend!" sputtered Flash. "I can't stand the guy! Look, just examine the thing, will you? You'll see—it's not mechanical, it's flesh and blood."

The bearded man looked interested. "It *is* astonishingly lifelike," he said. He turned to Harry. "Surely you won't object to our examining it."

"Sorry," said Harry. "I do object. Professional secrets, you know."

The other man had come down off the porch and was snapping pictures of me and Bluto.

"Please!" cried Harry. "I'm not yet ready to show this to the public."

The man shrugged and put down his camera. But he continued to walk around Bluto, nodding and shaking his head.

"Look at it!" cried Flash hysterically. "It's real, I tell you."

"Harry, I think you'd better let them examine the thing," said Peter.

Harry hesitated.

"That's an order," said Peter sharply.

We were distracted by a crashing sound as something new came thundering up the trail.

Chapter Sixteen

Back to the Past

It was Brenda. She was riding Betsy the Behemoth. Winnie was walking along beside her, holding the control box.

Harry began to smile. "I'll let you examine that one," he said. "It doesn't have as many of my professional secrets."

"Not that one!" cried Flash. "That one's a fake. The Tyrannosaurus rex is the real one."

That sank it for Flash. The idea that one dinosaur was a robot and one was real was too much for anyone to believe—even if it was the truth. I was sure that once the reporter and the scientist had had a chance to examine Betsy, they would be convinced that Bluto was a robot, too.

Brenda slid off Betsy and came over to stand next to me.

"We've got to get back to Harry's lab *now*," she

said desperately. "If we don't get those dinosaurs moving soon, they'll miss the vortex."

"Harry," I said, "I think I'd better get this one out of here now, don't you?"

"Yes, definitely," he said and nodded.

With Robert directing Bluto, we headed back to the SFX shack.

I thought we had done a great job convincing the scientist and the reporter that the dinosaurs were fakes. But when we gathered up Twitta and Dingbat and went to the cliff, we found that the man with the beard had followed us.

"You kids may have fooled the others," he said. "But you can't fool me. That Tyrannosaurus rex is real, and we all know it."

"What makes you think that?" I asked. I tried to sound bold and defiant, but I don't think I quite carried it off.

"Because in the ten years I've been studying those animals I've found some major errors in the way we've been thinking about them. This so-called model doesn't have any of those errors. It *does* have all the features my studies have turned up over the last few years—things no one but me knows about. Therefore, I conclude that it's real."

"Are you going to take it away to study?" asked Brenda.

"I can't think of anything in the world I would like better," said the man. His eyes glittered with a kind of greed. But he sighed and said, "Unfortunately, it all depends."

"On what?" I asked.

"On where it came from."

"It came from the past," I said.

The man turned pale. "I was afraid you might say that."

"You believe me?" I asked in surprise.

"Why shouldn't I?"

"I don't know," I said. "It's not very—scientific."

The man smiled. "It's not very scientific to ignore reality. The reality I see is three dinosaurs that have no right to be here. But they're here. So they must have gotten here somehow."

"I don't get it," said Winnie. "If you knew they were real, why didn't you say something back at the main office?"

The man rubbed his face. "I didn't become a scientist to take all the wonder out of the world. I went into science *because* the world is so wonderful, and I want to help protect it."

"Are you saying you'll help us get them back?" I asked.

"What choice do I have? Either we get them

back, or the world is going to start changing around our ears."

I stared at him in astonishment. "You know about reality shifts?" I asked.

He laughed. "I read a lot of science fiction. It prepares you to deal with the real world."

I wasn't sure that science fiction would prepare him to deal with Robert. But then, it didn't seem likely that Robert would show himself to a fourth mortal, so I decided not to worry about it.

"Aren't you going to ask us how we got them here?" asked Brenda.

The man smiled. "Would you tell me if I did? Could I force you to tell me if you don't want to?"

I blinked. I wasn't used to an adult being so reasonable. As if to demonstrate how odd it was, Flash showed up, being an unreasonable bully.

"What do you think you're doing, Stuart?" he screamed. "Trying to make a fool of me?"

"That would be like making a duck out of a duck," said Robert.

Flash headed toward Twitta. "I'm taking this one back to camp, and I don't want anyone trying to stop me."

"Flash," said Brenda, "they have to go home now."

"Don't be stupid," said Flash. "They don't have to go anywhere except to a museum." He paused. "Look, if you guys will stop trying to screw it up, I'll even cut you in on the deal. I'll take the biggest cut, of course, since I'm the one who arranged it. But there's enough to go around. You'll be rolling in dough."

"That won't do us any good if the reality shift hits," I said.

"The what?" asked Flash.

"Winnie, tell him about it," I said.

Winnie tried. He really did. Flash listened for about fifteen seconds, then said, "Oh, shut up, you little weenie."

Winston turned red, but he kept talking. "If we don't send those dinosaurs back, there's no telling what might happen," he said. "And according to my calculations, this is the time and place to do it."

Of course, that was only a matter of Winnie calculating out what Robert had told us. But there was no sense in trying to explain all that to Flash.

Nor was there any time. Actually, Time with a capital T was the problem, because as I looked across the lake, I could see the time vortex heading right for us.

"There it is!" I cried. "Come on, we've got to get these guys to the shore."

"Don't move," said Flash in a commanding voice. To my astonishment, he had pulled a gun on us.

"Flash!" said Winnie. "Look behind you!"

Flash laughed. "How dumb do you think I am?"

I wasn't about to answer that question while he was holding a gun!

The vortex was getting closer. I wondered if it would snatch Flash into the past—or the future. I had a feeling that reality was teetering on the brink of destruction.

Then three things happened, almost at the same moment.

First, Bluto went nuts. I think it was fear. The time vortex was approaching, weaving back and forth across the water. When Robert told him he had to step into it, Bluto started to roar in terror.

Second, Flash took advantage of the confusion to snatch Twitta and run into the forest.

Third, we found out that Winnie was wrong. You *could* see the reality shift when it hit.

Chapter Seventeen

The Shift Hits the Fan

I think it was Flash running off with the dinosaur that started it. When he did that the chances of getting Twitta home dropped sharply. In that instant the world started to melt around us. Trees twisted, changed colors, changed back; they stretched up, then shrank down, as if they couldn't decide what shape they were going to be.

The ground began to swell and sink beneath us. It heaved up and down as if something were breathing underneath it.

Dark forms appeared in the sky. They disappeared, came back, then disappeared again, flickering in and out of existence.

Brenda started to say something; a long forked tongue flicked out of her mouth.

Clearly, reality just wasn't what it used to be.

112

"Robert," I screamed. "We've got to do something!"

"You'd better do it," said an old man sitting on the ground in front of me. He looked oddly familiar.

"Robert?" I asked in astonishment.

He nodded. "In the flesh," he said.

"I don't get it."

"I didn't get it either—the bullet that killed me, that is. I'm still alive!"

I blinked. If in the new reality Robert was still alive, then sending the dinosaurs back would send him back to being dead.

"Don't even think about it," said Robert. His face was starting to grow scales. "We've *got* to put things back the way they were."

I tried not to scream again. I reached toward my own face, then pulled my hand away, afraid of what I might find.

"You've got to catch Flash," said Robert.

"But how? He's too far ahead of me. I can't run that fast."

"Take me," said a new voice.

I turned around and almost fell over. The voice came from Dingbat!

"How—" I started to ask.

"Shut up and climb on," he commanded.

113

I didn't need to be told twice. I jumped on his back and we galloped after Flash.

We hadn't traveled more than a few yards when the ground stopped shaking. The trees were still shifting, but more slowly.

"We're past the center of the change area," said Dingbat. "But it will be stretching this way soon, spreading like a ripple on a pond."

I could see what he meant when a five-foot-long squirrel galloped across the path in front of us.

"How come you can talk?" I asked. I clung to his neck as he bent forward and ran even faster.

"When you start taking reality apart at the seams, anything can happen," he said. "Especially if you happen to be standing at the center of the process."

The ground heaved underneath us and almost knocked us over. Suddenly I spotted them. "Over there!" I cried, pointing off to our left.

Flash was huddled under a tree. He had Twitta tucked in his lap. They were both looking around with wide and terrified eyes.

I leapt off Dingbat and ran across the flexing earth. My first plan was to snatch the baby triceratops out of Flash's arms. My backup plan

114

was to reason with him, but I didn't figure that would do much good.

What wasn't in my plans at all was the fact that when Flash took one look at me he started to scream as if he were seeing the end of the world.

"Take it!" he cried. "Take it! Just leave me alone, you monster!"

I blinked. I wondered what I looked like, and decided that I didn't want to know. I was terrified enough as it was. What if the vortex was gone when we got back? I knew the changes we were experiencing right then were only pebbles on the mountain of changes that would come if we didn't set things right.

My stomach was churning with fear. Clutching Twitta, I ran back to Dingbat. I kept thinking I was going to blink out of existence at any second.

"Climb on," he said. "Climb on—and hold tight!"

Bending forward, Dingbat ran straight and smooth, like an arrow, back to the clearing.

All hell had broken loose at the edge of the lake. An eruption of sound and light swirled around us.

"Give me Twitta," demanded Dingbat.

I climbed off his back and tucked Twitta into

his outstretched hands. He shot forward and disappeared into the vortex. But the reality shift still howled and whirled around us.

Then I realized that Bluto was still standing near us. He wasn't happy. In fact, he was crying.

"I can't do it," he blubbered. "I just can't face that thing."

Standing in front of the weeping twenty-foot-tall monster was a pudgy-looking lizard boy. It took me a second to realize it was Winnie!

"Don't be such a wimp!" said Winnie. "I've looked up to you all my life. Now you get up and get in there while you still can, or who knows what might happen."

"Yes, sir," sniffed Bluto. He shook his massive head and started to walk toward the vortex. At the edge, he stopped.

"*Go!*" shrieked Winnie.

Bluto stepped into the vortex—and everything stopped. The howling was gone. The ground stopped shifting. Reality snapped into place so fast it made my head ring.

I looked around. Winnie and Brenda were normal-looking. Robert had disappeared altogether. The scientist was clutching a tree, staring at the world with wide eyes and a big grin.

116

"We made it!" he screamed with glee. "It's over!"

I nodded grimly. I only had one question—a question the scientist couldn't answer.

Where was Robert?

Chapter Eighteen

Pebbles in a Pond

First thing next morning, Harry started to re-write the script for *Day of the Dinosaur*. Of course, if you saw the movie, you already know that.

Only now you know the rest of the story.

As for Flash, he had to go stay in a hospital for a while. He never did have a good grip on reality, at least not the reality that counts, things like friends and family and trying to do the right thing. So he needed to do something simple for a while, like sit and watch a goldfish bowl, before he could face the world again.

Which meant that things were back to normal at camp.

Too normal, as a matter of fact.

Robert was still missing.

After the second day I began to get really nervous. Had something happened to him?

Almost a week after our adventure, Brenda, Winnie, and I went up to the small cliff where the last time vortex had hit. We sat on a log, staring at Misty Lake and talking about the things that had happened, about time vortexes and reality chains, and wondering how the things we did would change the world to come.

I threw a pebble into the water.

"Better be careful," said a voice behind me. "When you throw a pebble into the water, you can never tell just where the ripples might end up."

"Robert!" I cried. "I've been worried about you!"

"Sorry," he said. "I needed to go think for a while."

"Uh-oh. Now I'm *really* worried."

"Stuart Glassman, boy comedian," said Robert. But he said it nicely.

"What were you thinking about?" asked Brenda.

Robert grimaced. "Me," he said. "I had a horrible experience when that reality shift hit. I had to deal with a temporary reality where I hadn't died."

"What's so horrifying about that?" I asked. "Didn't you like being alive?"

Robert looked at me. "I loved it," he said in the most serious voice I had ever heard him use. "Being alive is *wonderful*."

120

"I get it," said Winnie. "It was going back to being dead that was so awful."

I nodded. I had been wondering about that, and feeling really bad for Robert.

But he surprised me. "That was no problem," he said. "I'm used to being dead. Happens to everyone sooner or later, you know. You live and then you die. It's not such a big deal."

"Well, then, what was so awful?" cried Brenda.

Robert closed his eyes and did his shivering trick.

"I didn't like the way I turned out," he said.

I laughed.

Robert shook his head sadly. "Don't laugh too hard, Stuart," he said. "It can happen to anyone. That's what I came back to tell you. Be very careful you don't grow up to be a jerk." He paused for a moment. Then he smiled at me. "Well, kid," he said at last, "see you on the other side."

He began to disappear.

"Robert!" I cried.

His voice came out of the empty air. "So long, Stuart. Have a nice life!"

For a while no one said anything. Finally Winnie threw another pebble into the water.

We sat there and watched the ripples spreading toward the shore.

About the Author and Illustrator

Bruce Coville has written dozens of books for young readers, including *My Teacher is an Alien, Monster of the Year*, and the Camp Haunted Hills books, *How I Survived My Summer Vacation* and *Some of My Best Friends Are Monsters*. He grew up in central New York, where he's lived most of his life. Before becoming a full-time writer, Bruce Coville worked as a magazine editor, a teacher, a toymaker, and a gravedigger.

John Pierard is best known for his illustrations for *Isaac Asimov's Science Fiction Magazine, Distant Stars*, and several books in the *Time Machine* series. He lives in Manhattan.